The Pit

Andrew Fordham

Thank you for buying my book – I really hope you enjoy reading it.
When you have finished and if you have time, could you please leave a review on the Amazon site.

You can find out more about my series of books at :
Andrew Fordham : Amazon Author Page

I really enjoy engaging with readers of my books, and have set up a blog page on my website which I invite you to join.

Over time, I will give insights into my writing process - such as characterisation, settings, and plot research, and will also use the Blog page to keep readers informed of my upcoming new books and series.

You can sign up at :

Andrew Fordham : Blog

I hope to see you there !

ISBN 9798425159380

It's great being your own boss on a summer morning, working outside as the early mist is starting to burn off.

Even so, I sometimes miss the easy days of working for someone else and letting them have all the headaches.

The ringing of my spade against stone signalled that it probably wasn't going to be an easy day.

A woman had stopped about 40 yards away to clear up after her dog. Nice.

I recalled seeing her in the village once or twice. Maybe in the pub. I think she was from one of those families who have been here since the year dot.

She never really spoke, normally just gave a slight dip of the head, to acknowledge my existence.

"Morning love. Good weather for it," me trying to be all friendly like.

"For what?" she looked confused.

"Just being outside really."

"If you say so," as she stood there, bag in hand.

"Well, you're not alone."

"Alone? In what?" She looked even more confused now.

Did she think I meant collecting dog crap?

"Being outdoors. It's going to be a glorious day," me being all local yokel type.

She finished tying the bag and slipped it into her pocket. Nice, again.

"And a busy day for walkers," I added.

She looked over towards where I had nodded, then back at me, as if I was the village idiot.

With a shrug and a half-smile, she tugged on the Springer and turned away.

I'm well known in the village, and beyond, Tim Benson - Handyman and Small Works Builder; but even after living here for nearly a decade I still feel like an outsider.

I looked over towards the other side of the field, where I was sure I had seen someone less than a minute ago.

No one there now.

Odd, as there is nothing on that side of the field but a low fence and then other fields, so nothing to be hidden by, and nowhere to hide.

In the two days I'd already spent here, the dog walker lady was the first person I'd seen - well, her and now the other one.

Not surprising really, as the field is on the northern extremity of the village.

Known to the locals as Lammas Land, the field isn't used much now. The whole area gets waterlogged, so people tend to avoid it, and it doesn't help that the access track is heavily potholed.

Lammas Land is a strange term, and one I'd never come across before moving here.

According to my mate Jacko who is into local history and such things, it means a field or meadow given by the church, or a local landowner, for the exclusive use of the village residents.

A bit like common land I suppose, and now under the auspices of our parish council.

The village cricket team used to play here, but they disbanded a few years before I arrived.

However, cricket is now back in fashion, and the council wants to be seen to be fashionable.

Hence me being asked to put in a quote for installing land drains in the corner of the field where the track ends so that it can be used for car parking.

Hopefully, a new generation can delight at the crack of leather on willow and salivate at the thought of tasty tea-time cucumber sarnies.

'The Oval' it won't be, but it could be a nice place, nonetheless.

I really want to make a good impression with the parish council as it's taken me four years to get onto their register of approved contractors, and this job could be my way of accessing the rest of the contract.

Might be a nice little earner, mending the potholes, refurbishing the scoreboard and sightscreens, and building a new pavilion - well it's a large shed really.

This part of the job had to be finished by Monday and I had allowed myself four days. It had been going well, and I still had today and Sunday left, but - now I had the stone to deal with.

It was only about a foot below the surface, and I immediately knew what it was - a piece of stone debris from one of the local buildings destroyed during the reign of Henry VIII. He of the six wives.

In the Middle Ages there used to be several important religious sites hereabouts, until Henry fell out with the church in Rome and decided to demonstrate his displeasure by demolishing the abbey, several churches, priories, and the like.

The people of Wickham Parva are always digging this stuff up in back gardens and on allotments, but I've never heard of anyone coming across a piece this far out of the village.

They say you should leave the stones where they are found. Apparently, it's bad karma to move them.

It didn't take me long to discover another six pieces, and I started to question my business acumen and the profit-driven decision-making process which led me to price the job on a dig-out by hand basis, rather than including the cost of hiring a mini-excavator.

I might be in my fifth decade now, but I've looked after myself, and as none of the individual stones looked too big, I could bring the truck closer, load them on and get rid of them later.

Well, if I wanted to make a good impression and get paid by the end of the month, I needed to get my invoice in on Monday, and the job wouldn't finish itself so I'd better . . . .

"Hello?"

I was sure I'd heard footsteps behind me.

I spun around quickly. Too quickly, as my glasses slipped and sat precariously on the tip of my nose, leaving me unable to focus properly.

But I could focus enough to see a figure in the half-distance, fading into what remained of the morning mist.

That was a bit weird.

Sitting here on the corroded wheel assembly of one of the dilapidated cricket sightscreens, I was trying to roll a cigarette.

My fingers were sweaty - and quivering slightly, although it wasn't that hot yet, as it was still a couple of hours until midday.

I'd already ruined two of the thin pieces of gummed paper and dropped at least one cigarette's worth of tobacco on the grass.

I was starting to get the feeling someone else was here. Was I being watched?

I know I don't always put every cash job through the books, and technically I ought to be VAT registered, but I'm small fry compared to the multinational businesses who seem to get away with murder when it comes to paying taxes.

Would the authorities really be bothered about me? Perhaps I ought to be a bit careful for a while.

The feeling of uneasiness started to subside as I felt the smoke fill my lungs.

Yes, it's a bad habit - it's not the only one I have - and I know it can kill you.

But at certain times I find that a roll-up is comforting. I can't explain it. I have no excuses.

Anyway, tea break over, I ought to get on and dig those stones out and load them onto my truck.

I might even be able to sell them to the local garden centre, so that those well-to-do villagers living in the big houses near the church could use them to decorate their perfectly manicured grounds.

I didn't think I needed to notify the parish council about my discovery, they would only want official forms completed - probably in triplicate.

These old stones are commonplace enough, and the local museums and heritage centres have scores of sketches and photographs, so these few were unlikely to be missed.

And I really did need to finish this job so I could get an invoice into the council after the weekend.

"Sorry about that, but needs must . . ." I had to shout, as the reception in the field was rubbish.

My mobile phone is a bit ancient as well.

"Yep, we can meet there this evening if you want to - but it will have to be a quick one. Okay, bye."

Good. I'd managed to put off my afternoon session with Jacko until this evening.

When Jacko wants a pint, he rarely means just the one.

I should be able to get most of the heavy work finished off this afternoon if I put my back into it, so a few pints this evening would be something to look forward to.

Well, that was the sit-rep, an hour ago.

But now I had a different problem. Well, the same problem, but on a different scale.

The carved ecclesiastical stones were all safely on my flatbed truck and covered with a tarpaulin to shield them from prying eyes.

Now, in the earth directly below where I had removed the stone blocks, was a stone slab.

Same type of material - limestone I would guess.

This thing was huge though - compared to the stones - probably about three feet wide, five feet long and six inches thick.

I'm sure I read somewhere that limestone weighs in at about two tons per cubic yard - or thereabouts - so, that would make this slab a tad over half a ton.

That's in proper English weights and measures. None of your fancy Euro measures for me.

I like my beer in pints, and my tobacco in ounces.

Anyway, half a ton, or even 500 kilograms, was too heavy for me to handle on my own without ropes, or a pulley, or a winch.

But moving it was not my main concern.

Covered in intricate carvings and stylised motifs, to my mind it looked important.

And in the world I inhabit, 'important' can often be translated as 'problem'.

That was one big lump of stone, and it had to be moved.

My idea was to use the winch on the front bumper of my truck to pull it out.

But I couldn't even get it raised an inch or two to get the rope under, so that was a no go.

Beads of sweat had formed on my forehead, part exertion and part sunshine as the day was starting to heat up, and the air wasn't moving. Just as a normal summer's day should be.

That's what made the chilly draught I felt on the back of my neck so strange.

That, and the silence.

A silence so intense that I could almost hear it.

As though every noise had been sucked away.

And the birds - pigeons I think - were not flying over the field. It seemed like they were skirting the boundaries, flying around it.

I'd heard that homing pigeons had a superior sense of direction. But these were just ordinary wood pigeons.

Do they do that?

I know that animals and birds react to things we can't even sense.

Must be a storm brewing.

Possible bad weather and bonkers pigeons aside, my immediate concern was the monolith in front of me. How did Stonehenge ever get built? Not by middle-aged builders, that's for sure.

I couldn't tell the council about this now, even though the carvings on the slab were probably important. They would have the beardy archaeologists crawling all over this place with their tape measures, clipboards, and tie-dye tee shirts. I would never get my invoice in then.

Probably best if I covered it up and let some intrepid archaeologists make their name in the future, by discovering it all anew.

Anyway, I was sure I'd seen something on *Time Team* where they had developed non-intrusive techniques to examine remains whilst still in the ground. Some sort of radar, I think.

Yep. Good idea. Cover it up. Problem solved.

"So, this is where you've been hiding."

"Jeeeez!" I blurted. And probably an octave higher than normal.

Jacko had turned up unexpectedly.

"How do you do that?" as I purposely deepened my tone.

"Do what? Sneak up on you? Easy!" he smirked.

"You okay then?" I wasn't sure why he was here.

"Yep. Just thought I'd bring you one of these."

He handed me a can of Brew Dog. Our favourite hangover in a can. Nine percent of Britain's finest.

"Ta. Maybe in a while. I really have got to finish here before it gets too hot. I'm melting already."

"I'll give you a hand. I've got nothing better to do."

He laid his bike down on the grass.

"So, what we are doing?" He picked up a shovel and I couldn't imagine anyone looking more like an 18th-century navvy than Jacko.

Scruffy git.

Torn trousers, stained shirt and a pork-pie hat which had probably had at least three previous owners.

Forty going on twenty. And two stone overweight.

He looks just like a typical mature student. Because that's what he is.

I think he's four years into his six year part-time online degree in 'English Church Architecture'.

Spends all his spare time in the local churches doing brass rubbings and charcoal sketches of architectural details.

A true born local, he's never moved away.

He was the first person I met when I arrived in Wickham Parva, and we just clicked.

"Got to finish backfilling that trench, and then lay the pipe and backfill the other trench over there." I pointed out the two lengths of extended trench.

By lengthening the two original trenches I had achieved the same overall length of land drain, thereby meeting the terms of the contract with the parish council.

He started straight away, and before long the two of us had the job nearly done.

We were sweating like proverbial pigs and decided to take a breather.

"So, you been tracking me then?" I mopped my brow with my sleeve.

"How do you mean?"

"I saw you a couple of times earlier, over there," I pointed to the other side of the field, "trying to do your Ninja warrior thing, creeping up on me."

"Not me mate. You need to take more water with it or wear a hat to stop sunstroke," he said, with a broad smile.

Picking up a road-pin which I had been using to set out the line for the trenches, he wielded the four feet long half-inch diameter steel rod over his head like a warrior's sword.

"Bollocks! It was you, I know it was. Freaked me out for a bit though."

He didn't bother to answer, but just shook his head and wandered over to his bike and picked up a can of beer from the shade of the basket.

He ripped back the ring-pull and kicked at some rubble.

He was standing right over the area where I had discovered the stone slab, and although I had back-filled the hole with earth taken from the other trenches and compacted it as best I could, it was still fairly obvious that the area had been recently disturbed.

He finished his beer with three deep gulps, threw the can on the ground, swung the road-pin around his head again and then with both hands thrust it down.

It was quite impressive really, straight through the middle of the can.

"There can be only one," he said in an unbelievably bad Sean Connery accent from *Highlander*, as he continued pushing the steel rod through the foot-and-a-half of loosely compacted earth, until it stopped with a jolt.

"Crikey! There's something down there," as he dropped to his knees and started to paw at the earth, "it felt solid, like rock."

I didn't know what to do, or what to say.

So I did nothing, and said nowt.

It took him less than a minute to dig a small hole with his hands, down to the surface of the slab, exposing a ten-inch diameter section.

"Look at this, Tim, it's stone and covered with carvings. Probably medieval. I'm sure I've seen similar motifs before. Give me a hand and we can see how big this is."

He reached over to where the shovel stood upright in the ground.

"What's up? You don't seem very excited about this. It could be an important find."

Giddy like a schoolboy, he was.

"Hey, we might even get on the telly. Interviewed. That blonde bird on the news channel, you know, the one with the perfect . . . Oy! I was about to use that!"

I snatched the shovel away from him and walked over to the hole he had dug and started to fill it in.

"What are you doing that for?"

"Listen," I turned to face him, "that needs to stay hidden, at least for now."

"But it might be something really . . . huge! You know, like one of them hordes of treasure that get discovered in random fields, or even something like Sutton Hoo."

I raised my eyebrows at him.

"Might be. You don't know. And we won't know unless we dig it out."

"I know, but not now. Trust me. Please." I tried to reason with him, but he still looked fairly determined.

I needed to calm him down a bit.

"I see you've got your bag with you. Got the brass rubbing kit?"

He nodded.

"So, we dig out a bit more earth, you do a quick rubbing, we cover the whole thing again, then head to the Black Bull and talk it through over a couple of pints."

I could see the cogs whirring in his brain.

"Okay. If you're buying?"

Works every time.

Lunchtimes at the Black Bull were often quiet, and today was no exception.

It's a proper English village pub with exposed beams, inglenook fireplace, and oak furniture, which caters to the occasional visitor from outside the village, and whilst happy to take their money is equally happy to see them leave.

The village is prone to flooding when we get heavy rain and the river bursts its banks, so all the buildings have a high set of steps at their entrances. We waited outside briefly whilst one of the regulars negotiated the step down, his dodgy hip joint giving him a slight problem.

The pub probably hasn't changed much in the two or three centuries it's been the centrepiece of the village. Originally a coaching inn, the bricks are a deep burnt yellow and the recently renewed roof of dark orange clay peg tiles has weathered beautifully.

It's summertime, so whilst there was no welcoming heat or wood smoke from the inglenook fireplace, the aroma of hops and pork scratchings was unmissable.

As well as the bar area, there are two main rooms. Both imaginatively named.

From the Front Room we could hear the click of dominoes being laid down in what passes for our most competitive local sport. The Black Bull have been area champions for as long as anyone can remember.

We headed for the Back Room, normally the busier of the two during the evening sessions, but often empty during the day. Which was how we found it.

All in all, the pub was a no-frills haven from the crap that is modern life. And we loved it that way.

Mike, the Landlord, isn't stuck in the past though, and he does offer free wi-fi to his regulars.

Jacko had calmed down by now, and I gave him a tenner so he could collect our beers.

We didn't have to order as Mike knew what we wanted.

Two pints of best bitter, two pickled eggs, and two bags of unsalted crisps. Put the eggs in the with the crisps, shake the bag, and vinegar from the eggs flavours the crisps.

Lovely. *Master Chef* could learn a thing or two from the Black Bull.

I set up my tablet, which I always keep in the truck, finding the screen easier to view detailed construction drawings on than with a mobile phone.

We spent the next twenty minutes searching for any comparisons to the wax rubbings that Jacko had made of the exposed surface of the carved stone slab.

Couldn't find anything remotely close.

I had to have a pee, and on the way back, approaching our table from a different direction, I was able to view the wax rubbings the other way up.

It looked like a pattern of swords over stylised crosses to me.

Heavy, medieval type broad swords. Crosses with the ends of each arm splayed.

What a strange mix of motifs, military and religious.

Religious and military. Knights Templar?

That wouldn't be so outrageous, as this whole area is known to have been a religious hotbed for centuries.

In particular from the Norman Conquest up to the Reformation, a period of 500 years.

In the middle of that period were the Knights Templar, who were disbanded in the early 14th century.

And it's well known that they had a preceptory on the outskirts of Wickham Parva.

Actually, it was in Wickham Magna, which doesn't exist any longer.

During one of the many plagues which swept Europe in the Middle Ages, the village of Wickham Magna was decimated, whilst its neighbour Wickham Parva was more fortunate.

The result being that Wickham Parva, or Little Wickham, is now the name used for the surviving settlements of both villages.

Much research has been done over the years on the Templars and their association with the local area, and we found a wealth of information in the local history section of the parish council website.

The Templars had several successful farming enterprises, in both Wickham Magna and Wickham Parva, and grew a variety of crops.

They would store their surplus grain and root vegetables in underground pits, and seal them with stone slabs. Only they would know the location, thereby denying the church or any local bigwigs the opportunity of stealing their hard-won produce.

Winters were severe then, and not everyone set aside crops for the long months of darkness and cold. It wasn't only for their legendary treasure that the Templars were the object of jealousy.

The storage pits were not a typical device used by the Templars, and it seems that in this area they improved existing pits from the late Saxon and early Norman period, at least 200 years old, even then.

There have been a number of other pits discovered within a 10-mile radius - used and reused right through to the 16th and even 17th centuries - but none with an intact stone slab sealing the entrance.

So we might be onto a winner, at least for the beardy archaeologists anyhow.

I strolled to the bar to get another round in, and when I got back Jacko had followed a link to the Environment Agency water table records, which showed that the previously discovered pits had all been abandoned in the past because they flooded.

The builders of the old Abbey - who, according to Jacko, had previously built our local church - diverted the course of one of the feeder streams for the local river so that they could create a couple of fishponds. This had the effect of silting up the river, which caused it to burst its banks when we had heavy rain, thereby flooding the valley floor and the adjacent fields.

So I might have stumbled across a medieval grain storage pit - probably full of water.

Cosmic.

Well, here we were again, back at Lammas Land.

All I wanted was to get paid for the council job, but Jacko had a proper hard-on over the Templars and wanted to search for treasure.

I knew he would want to come back here - even if it was on his own - so probably best if I tagged along for the ride.

The storm, if indeed there was ever going to be one, had never arrived. But the air still felt stifling and oppressive, as though there was a change in the offing.

Jacko was sitting on the mound of earth we had excavated an hour earlier.

We had dug out an additional seven foot at one end and about three foot at the other, so now we had a shallow trench the width of the slab and about 15 foot long.

"Go on then, amaze me. How are we going to do this?"

I had collected three lengths of 6 x 2-inch sawn timber, each about four foot long, from my lock-up on the other side of the village, half a dozen concrete paving blocks - the type used on driveways - and a couple of five-foot scaffold tubes which had flattened ends.

"It looks as though the slab is sitting on a stone cill, so we should be able to get the flat end of these steel poles in between them and lift it enough to slip the blocks in. Then do the same on the other side."

I had given it a bit of thought, and decided this should work, particularly with two of us.

"Then we can repeat the operation at the other end, so the slab is sitting on four blocks, one on each corner. We can put the other two in the middle of each long side for extra support.

 Then run the rope under the slab, lengthways, wrap it around at least a couple of times and fix the end with the metal eyelet to the winch on the truck and . . . well, hopefully that will work."

Listening to myself, I now wasn't 100% confident it would work. But I couldn't think of anything else.

"Simples!" Jacko, pretending to be one of those meerkats from the TV adverts.

And, simples it was. Thankfully.

Fifteen minutes later, after moving one pair at a time, the concrete blocks were still under the slab; but now in the seven-foot extended trench.

We had placed the lengths of timber under the blocks to stop them sinking into the earth, and stood back to admire our handiwork, quite pleased with ourselves. And rightly so.

Perhaps a couple of middle-aged builders could have erected Stonehenge after all.

But they would have had to wait 5,000 years for the invention of a Self-Contained Underwater Breathing Apparatus, commonly known as SCUBA, if they wanted to know what was in the pit.

For it was, as we had half-expected, full of water.

Well, not quite full, as the water was perhaps three feet short of the stone cill upon which the slab had sat.

"It must drain naturally then."

"What?" I looked at Jacko.

"It drains naturally. No smell, and it's not stagnant", he explained, as he leaned over the edge to inspect the inner rim of the entrance shaft.

He had to be be right, because even though the water was a bit murky it looked as though the blocks of stone which formed the walls, or maybe they were chalk, didn't have any waterlevel stains.

They were uniformly weathered with age, which would indicate that the water level did in fact rise and fall naturally in the pit as the water table was affected by the flooding and draining of the land around it.

"Naturally draining or whatever, it's a good job we bought the pump," he added.

After Jacko had found the information on the Environment Agency website, we asked Mike the Landlord if we could borrow his petrol generator and water pump, which he keeps for the odd times that his cellar floods.

Jacko was rubbing his hand over the blocks forming the entrance shaft, which was itself quite narrow.

Circular, and certainly no more than about two foot in diameter, it would be difficult for a man to get in. And then out again. They probably used to send in children.

I peered in and could just make out what was presumably the curve of the wall of a main chamber which started about six inches above the water line.

No way in there then. Not without pumping it out first.

"Hey, look at this," Jacko was now using his soiled old handkerchief on the stone cill upon which the cover slab had been seated, "there are carved marks on this stone."

Indeed, there were.

He fetched his bag with the brass rubbing kit he used in his Church Architecture studies.

With his pork-pie hat and the canvas bag, he looked like a chunky 5' 8" version of Indiana Jones.

"What are you laughing at?" He seemed quite indignant.

"Oh, nothing really . . . " I was still smiling.

He ignored me as he placed a sheet of his special paper over the carvings and then started to rub the paper with what looked like a block of wax.

The images appearing on the paper were much clearer than those on the stone itself, which I suppose is the whole point of the exercise.

I rolled myself a cigarette while he carried on, and by the time I'd smoked it he had about a dozen sheets covered in a crude tessellated border comprised of dots and cross-hatched lines.

We sat on the mound of excavated earth for a while, just looking at the rubbings.

"So, what do you reckon?" I was now quite intrigued about the pit. "Shall we pump it out?"

Jacko nodded. "How long do you think it'll take?"

"Well, it's a high-volume pump, and if this pit is roughly the same size as the others that have been found, then I reckon a couple of hours should do it."

"Enough time for us to have a peep inside before it gets dark then." I wasn't sure if he was asking a question or making a statement.

"Should be," I glanced at my watch, "its only ten past five."

"We'd better crack on then."

Which we did, and within 20 minutes we had the generator puffing away nicely, the pump doing its thing, and the large bore pipe discharging the water behind the old cricket scoreboard, a good 30 yards from the pit and on a slight downward gradient.

The pump was working quicker than I expected, and at just over the hour the noise coming from the outlet pipe changed from a gurgling of splashing water to a sludgy, muddy splosh.

The sun was moving towards the horizon but still about halfway up in the sky, however the narrowness of the entrance shaft and the curve of the walls below it limited the amount of natural light getting in.

We needed a torch to see properly inside the pit, and even then it was difficult to make out details.

But from our restricted viewpoint, we worked out that the pit was probably similar in size to the others found locally and seemed to be in good condition.

At a guess, it was 25 foot in diameter and 15 foot deep from the base of the entrance shaft down to the exposed floor level.

It was shaped like a bell and the walls were cut out of the natural chalk which forms the substrate throughout most of this part of the country, with the neck of the entrance shaft made of individually-cut chalk blocks.

The torchlight was reflected back, so it was still wet down there, with hopefully only surface mud remaining.

But at least we had pumped all the water out - so we wouldn't drown.

That was the next big question. Who was going in?

Easy one to answer really. Me.

There was no way that 'Chunkyana Jones' was ever going to squeeze through that narrow entrance shaft.

I'm six foot tall, just, but I've a slim frame and have kept in shape. I still have the same waist and chest measurements I had when I was 20.

We hitched up a rope to the winch on the truck bumper bar, and I fashioned a double bowline on the other end.

I'd seen a similar thing done by a steeplejack on a TV programme when he climbed an old industrial chimney, one loop around his chest and under the armpits, and the other loop under his butt, together forming a type of seat with harness.

He made quite a few programmes after that one, so it must have worked.

"You ready then?"

"Now or never, I guess!" I didn't feel as brave as I was trying to appear.

I sat on the edge of the shaft and after a couple of attempts we worked out how I could roll onto my belly, and Jacko could ease the rope and start to lower me while keeping the tension on, so I didn't drop like a stone.

My head was now level with the bottom of the entrance shaft and my legs and body were dangling inside the bell shape of the pit.

"Oy! If things go wrong, can I have your guitar?" Jacko, just being Jacko.

I craned my neck and was about to mouth an obscenity . . . who was that?

I could see Jacko framed by the rim of the pit entrance and silhouetted against the still bright sky. But who was that behind him?

It seemed as though I was looking past Jacko, and through a smeared pane of glass.

It looked like the outline of a person and I thought that I could make out a form - but no discernible features.

Was I seeing things - again?

Probably just the sunshine, so I squinted my eyes to focus better, and that's when I felt it.

My foot snagged on something.

My lace had snapped yesterday and the only spare I had was from some old boots, and it was probably twice as long as needed.

I had caught the over-large bow on a protruding nail earlier at my lock-up, so my first reaction was that I had snared my lace on something below me in the pit.

Perhaps something projecting from the interior which I hadn't seen from above because of the outward curve of the wall.

I tried to position my body so that I could look downwards, but I couldn't get my neck at the correct angle.

I looked up towards Jacko to get him to lower me another couple of feet.

He wasn't there.

No-one was there.

I called out. No answer.

I called out again. This time, I noticed, in a slightly higher pitch.

Still no answer.

I heard a squelching noise but couldn't decide if it was coming from above - or below.

Now I was starting to freak out a bit.

Quite a bit.

I heard the squelch again

I shouted for Jacko, this time bordering on a scream.

"What's the matter?"

I fell in love with his little round face peering over the edge, which almost immediately changed to rage.

"I've been shouting for you. Pull me up!"

"Never heard a thing - and I've been right here."

"Pull me up. Now!"

He disappeared again, but within seconds I heard the winch motor kick in and felt the rope tighten.

Then I was lying on the mud and grass surrounding the entrance shaft, staring up at the sky.

I lay there for a couple of minutes, composing myself.

Still no birds, I noticed.

Jacko walked over from the cricket scoreboard.

"You calmed down now? Proper little hissy fit you had back there." He nodded towards the pit entrance.

I had calmed down. Sort of.

"Where were you when I shouted?"

"I went for a pee but most of the time I was sitting right here," he pointed towards the edge of the pit, "and I never heard you shouting."

"Well, I did - a couple of times. And who was that with you?"

"Here we go again. There's been nobody else here. Just you and me. On our lonesomes."

"Well, I saw someone standing behind you."

"Make your bloody mind up - you just said that I wasn't there! Now you're saying there was two of us!" His little nostrils flared slightly.

I decided to leave it and started to remove the rope harness.

"So what were you just doing over there?" I pointed to the old cricket scoreboard.

"Oh, ahem, when I had a pee . . . I saw some pieces of bone in the mud that was bought up by the pump. I just went back for them."

A pee. Into the mud. Would that account for the sludgy squelching noise then?

"Bone?" I was intrigued, "Let's have a gander then."

They were only small fragments and they looked like animal bone to me. Not that I'm an expert.

"Well, I don't think there's any treasure here," I said with a half-laugh, "just a derelict storage pit."

I really didn't want to go back in there.

"I guess you're right," he said.

That surprised me. I thought Jacko would want to explore the pit now it was empty of water.

"Right? Yeah. Perhaps we ought to put the slab back and cover it with the earth again." I tried my luck.

"Agreed. Nothing more for us here," said with a slight hint of resignation, "and at least now you can put your invoice into the council and get paid."

Top bloke. Even through his disappointment, he was thinking of me. That's got to be worth another pint. Or two.

It didn't take too long to replace the slab, shovel in the earth, and re-lay the turf.

In a day or so, and after some of the long-awaited rain, the covered area would blend in quite well with the surroundings.

Back to the pub then.

It had been a long day, and I was starting to feel tired - probably why I was seeing things that weren't there.

I'm not ancient, I know, but I'm not a youngster either. Sometimes I forget that.

I was glad that we could put that earlier slight disagreement behind us. Jacko's my mate and I don't like to fall out with him.

He was on form and cracking a few jokes with the regulars in the Black Bull.

Although his jollity did seem forced, and I detected a nervousness in him.

On several occasions I caught him glancing towards me, or staring into a corner of the Back Room, into the shadows where Mike has never bothered to put a light.

I don't normally eat at the pub, but didn't fancy cooking this evening, so I'd ordered burger and chips from Mike's extensive bar menu.

Burger and chips, or if you fancied it, chips and burger. *Either one or go hungry* - that's what it says on the menu board.

I was squeezing some tomato sauce onto my chips when one of the regulars asked if anyone had more news about the road accident earlier in the afternoon.

Apparently, a van driver had hit someone on one of the roads that leads into the village, but when he stopped and walked back there was no one there.

Nice image - ketchup on chips. Blood on bones.

A couple from the village came in, shaking themselves off and shuffling their feet on the mat by the door, which then slammed shut behind them.

The loud crack of wood-on-wood made Jacko nearly spill his pint.

The couple were soaked, and someone made a quip about the storm finally arriving.

The woman commented that it was a storm like she hadn't known before. It had started about half an hour earlier - so we'd been lucky - with a dim light low in the sky on the other side of the village and the wind howling like someone in pain.

One of the blokes made a spooky wolf-howl noise, and we all laughed.

Except for Jacko, who asked the couple in which direction they saw the lights.

She pointed towards the window, in a vague northerly direction, towards the old playing field.

I felt Jacko glance towards me.

Mike came back from the cellar after changing a barrel, and placed his laptop on the bar, turning the screen towards us.

Well, it's his wife's laptop really. She spends most of her time on shopping channels, and according to him, most of his money as well.

She had been searching the Wickham Parva Community website for any interesting items for sale and had come across several blog entries posted by local residents during the last hour.

Some weird shit was going on out there.

Dogs going crazy - not just barking - but going off the scale.

One old chap near the church reckoned his ornamental pond had boiled, and he had posted a picture of fish floating among lily pads.

Another entry by a woman who claimed that her cast-iron fire pit, which she hadn't used for over a week, had heated up so much that the canvas cover had burst into flames.

It had been a hot day, but not that hot surely.

And yet Mike reckoned that in his cellar it was close to freezing, and he had to adjust the thermostat that controlled the barrel heat pads so that the beer didn't spoil.

The laptop pinged, and a little flag popped up in the corner of the screen indicating that additional posts had been sent. More strange stories.

I could see that all this talk had unsettled Jacko, and was surprised when he had one more mouthful, then put his half-finished pint on the bar and made his excuses.

Most unlike him, not to see a pint off properly.

I said I'd call him tomorrow, and he gave a thumbs up as he pulled on his hat and stepped out into the rain.

I reached over and poured the remains of his beer into my glass. Waste not want not, as my old dad would always say.

I hoped that I could count on Jacko to keep quiet about our discovery, at least until I got paid.

Some of the others took their lead from Jacko and the pub soon emptied, and as I didn't feel like drinking alone, I decided to head off too.

I can remember standing in the loo before leaving - otherwise I would never have made it home without having to find an unlit tree somewhere - and thinking that I'd seen the images on the rubbings from the cill stone around the pit entrance somewhere else.

And in my mind's eye I kept seeing the figure behind Jacko. Was it just my tiredness and the sunlight?

And the odd stuff happening around the village. Probably down to the stormy conditions.

Probably.

But what about the five thin, but deep, scratch marks on the side of my shoe?

There's nothing remarkable about St Saviour's.

It's a fairly typical 14th-century Norfolk village church with brick and flint external walls and a part-tiled, part-lead roof.

The current vicar is only the latest in a long line of incumbents who have each spent most of their tenure raising funds for repairs to this, repairs to that, and replacement of all the rest.

Me, I'm not much of a God-botherer. But I respect the right to believe, of those who do.

Jacko believes. I guess that's part of the reason why he studies what he does.

I did some work at St Saviour's once, making good a decorative window surround with resin and stone dust. The repairs might last a few years but will have to be done properly one day.

Another item for the fund-raising committee.

As I had arrived a little early, I was just sitting on a bench outside the church, admiring the view, and had overheard a couple of women clucking away about how the overnight storm hadn't been kind to the old building, and now the roof was missing some tiles and had developed a leak.

Apparently, it was deemed enough of a problem that the vicar had moved the Sunday services to a church in one of the nearby villages.

Poor Daphne wasn't pleased about the flower arrangements she did yesterday, and Marjorie didn't know if they had to take their own milk for the tea. They both agreed that the vicar could have given them more notice.

First World problems. Nothing like them to get the blood up.

I didn't think the Vicar would be too bothered though. The word was that he had friends in high places within the diocese.

I looked round as I heard the rapid crunch of gravel on the path.

"You're going to love this. Love it!" Jacko was beaming.

A complete change to his demeanour from the previous evening. That's what a good night's sleep does for you.

"Come on. Come on." He was bounding along like Tigger in *Winnie-the-Pooh*.

"Follow me. I've got the key."

He's been making brass rubbings and charcoal sketches in this, his local church, for a couple of years. I think it qualifies as the practical part of his degree.

The previous vicar was an old friend of his family, so when the new chap started last year, he was happy to continue letting Jacko have unrestricted access.

He had been somewhat cryptic in our earlier telephone conversation, so I didn't quite know what I was going to love.

I'm not sure where he was when he called, but the reception wasn't great, and when I broached the subject of yesterday's events, he didn't really want to talk about them. Just one of those days, he said, and to be fair I was glad to leave it at that.

Sometimes you can look too deeply into things that can be explained away quite rationally.

I think I was even starting to convince myself.

"So, what's with the rush?" as I tried to keep pace.

His little legs seemed as though they were going faster than his upper body, with the slapping of his trainers on the paved flooring breaking the peaceful calm of the ancient interior as the echo bounced back from the stone walls, which were remarkably clean after centuries of burning candle wax and incense.

I was sure he would tumble forwards in his excitement to get to the end of the long walkway through the church. The nave, I think it's called.

"You'll see. Amazing. You'll see!"

I hoped it was worth it. I'd been on a couple of Jacko's early morning 'Great Discovery' sessions before.

At the start of his degree, he found a lost tomb in the churchyard, by the fence which keeps the farm animals out. Turns out it was an upturned concrete water trough buried under sheep muck and stinging nettles. He was convinced that the rusting tins viewed through a crack in 'the tomb' were canisters holding priceless religious relics. We did find an old 1940's paintbrush though, which cleaned up nicely. I still use it.

Then there was the 'Case of the Morse Code Madonna'. A statue of the Virgin Mary inside the church from which tapping noises could be heard. Jacko was again convinced of his ability to unravel a mystery: the statue was sending messages to the faithful - via Morse Code. All I can say is that pre-Second World War heating pipes do rattle quite a lot.

"Have you been up all night?"

"Yep. I couldn't stop. It's all in the church records. You'll see."

He had stopped his half-running and was standing next to an ancient wooden box in one of the large alcoves which was at right angles to the nave. I recall it being called a transept, as it was in the opposite transept that I had repaired the window a couple of years back.

The box was standing on the stone floor and was a good size, at least six foot long, two foot square on section, and probably as old as the church.

The planks making up the sides were hewn oak, an inch and a half thick with a long-deceased carpenter's adze marks still visible on the surfaces, whilst the iron straps which girded the box had developed a distinct patination that was impossible to replicate, other than over time.

The lid, made of tooled leather bonded to oak planks fixed to a frame of elm, was open, and held back with iron pins and short lengths of chain with oversized links.

It was a wonderful piece of work, made more so by it still being in use some seven centuries after being crafted.

Stored inside were modern ring-binders and plastic boxes packed with index cards and other modern crud, which in truth was a bit disappointing.

A book full of illuminated manuscripts, or even a couple of vellum scrolls, would have been nice.

Jacko had dark rings under his eyes, and his hair was even more unkempt that usual, but this was all tempered by his air of excitement, something normally only observed in those with a true passion. With the possible exception of stamp collectors.

"Okay. Do you want the full-length explanation or the quick and dirty one?" he asked, still grinning.

"Go on, the quick one. And the quicker the better."

"Right. In those ring-binders are photocopies of most of the church records going back to the middle of the 17th century. So, that's nearly 300 years after the church was built. The original documents are in the local museum under lock and key."

He shuffled position as the morning sun was rising higher and shining through one of the large stained-glass windows directly into his eyes.

He continued, "Between 1790 and 1810 the church was repaired and modified. That's when the tiled roof replaced the thatched one."

"I didn't realise they used to have a thatched roof."

"Yeah, but not important. Concentrate!" He looked slightly fazed, so obviously I'd interrupted his flow.

He dipped into the box, picking up a cardboard folder brimming with loose leaves of paper. "In here, I found references to other, much earlier records. The originals of these papers must be somewhere, but these are copies, probably of earlier copies."

He turned and took a couple of paces to an alcove which I hadn't noticed before and pulled back the curtain to reveal a glass-fronted bookcase, the doors of which were already unlocked. He had no doubt been rummaging through those shelves as well as the box.

Dust motes caught in the sunlight, and I detected the unmistakable hint of fustiness and paper dust.

"Okay, still with me?" But he gave me no time to answer.

"Those papers led me to these records." He pulled out a hardbound book, which looked like something a Victorian clerk would have used to inscribe the interminably boring parish records in.

"And, this is where it all starts to get really interesting." He opened the record book.

"There's a date inside the front cover, 1871," he continued, "and a note stating that the contents are a true copy of various documents dating back to the time the church was built."

He passed me the book and I started reading as quickly as I could, but my brain had to adjust to reading the cursive handwritten script.

The text outlined how the land which now comprises Wickham Parva and the remnants of Wickham Magna was given by William I, the 'Conqueror', to one of the local Saxon Thanes, who was then knighted in the Norman tradition. They were clever like that, the Normans, getting the local landed gentry on their side to help govern.

The land was passed down, through the generations, father to son, until one of them decided to build a church.

I'm not sure if he just got up one morning and decided that was what he was going to do, but Sir Edward Wykham, as it was spelt in those days, did just that. He built a church. This one.

At the same time, this was about the mid 1370's, there was much unhappiness in 'Ye Merry Olde Englande'.

Punitive taxation to pay for unwanted foreign wars, and the social and economic meltdown from the Great Mortality, or Black Death, less than 40 years earlier.

And an unpopular half-French King who didn't know his arse from his elbow and who was heavily influenced by land-grabbing barons at home, and an interfering church in Rome.

Add to that the driving down of prices by imports from across the Channel, affecting the profitability of English farmers, craftsmen, and merchants.

It's no wonder there was some serious civil unrest in the shires.

And all of that a full six centuries before what modern historians like to call the 'Great European Experiment'.

Not that great really, and certainly not the only time the continent has tried to ensure peace through common trade objectives.

As the saying goes, 'There's nothing new under the sun'.

"Good, eh?" Jacko was bouncing around like he'd overdosed on E-numbers.

"Give me a chance. I've only just got to the bottom of the page. This style of handwriting is a bit hard to read."

The stone floor was sucking at my feet and making my legs ache, so I pulled out a small wooden stool from behind the curtain and sat down to continue reading.

Flipping over the page, in the margin I noticed a small, neatly drawn sketch of a medieval style hat with a feather in the brim. The feather had been coloured in and had faded over time, but there was still a hint of yellow.

I once took part in a pub quiz in which one of the questions was, 'Which royal house of England wore a yellow flowered shrub as one of its emblems?' Funny how you remember such odd facts.

So I knew that the King at the time the church was built was a Plantagenet, the royal house which in later history broke up into the two cadet branches of York and Lancaster, who between them properly buggered the country during the Wars of the Roses.

I thought it would be Edward III, but I was a few years out. It was in fact Richard II.

According to the unnamed author of the records, the King made one of his most loyal supporters, or probably more accurately one of his richest supporters, into a bishop.

Those were the times that you didn't really need to be all loved-up with God to be made a bishop. It was more of a political appointment to help keep order in the countryside you had control over.

And this new bishop certainly did that, for the common people were unhappy and the scent of rebellion was in the air.

Henry le Despenser, the newly made Bishop of Norwich, along with others of his ilk, helped King Henry put down the Peasants Revolt in this part of the country, by suppressing the yokels and farmhands who were armed to the teeth with their dangerous pitchforks, scythes, and oxen-drawn carts.

After all, the 'Fighting Bishop' - as he became known - only had men-at-arms with swords and maces, and full body chain and plate armour, bows and arrows, shields, and heavy cavalry with lances.

That's all these professional soldiers of an unpopular king had at their disposal to crush the upstart peasants, whose only real crimes were to want a better life for themselves and their kin, to benefit from the land they farmed, and to see those who ruled them contribute the same, voluntarily, as was forcibly taken from those they ruled, to pay for the wars fought on foreign soil in the name of the King.

I was getting unsettled by Jacko leaning over the record book to see how far I had progressed.

"I'm going out for a smoke. I'll take the book with me. Don't fret," I could see the alarm on his face, "I'll only be sitting on the bench."

Ten minutes later and cigarette finished, I was about to start reading again when I saw someone walking towards me.

The woman I had spoken to yesterday, with her Springer Spaniel. And, I noted, carrying another small plastic bag.

"Hello again." I closed the book.

She smiled, possibly thinking I was one of the big-house residents from this end of the village, taking the air and reading in the tranquil setting of the churchyard. But then, seeing it was one of the hoi polloi, she changed her expression into one of mild disdain, turned up her nose, and passed me by without any response.

I watched her strut off and smiled inwardly.

Silly cow.

No wonder the East Anglians rose up against your type.

Back to the record book.

After several smaller skirmishes and with the tide of rebellion ebbing and flowing, the final showdown came during the glorious summer of 1381, at the Battle of North Walsham in the County of Norfolk, when the King's supporters slaughtered hundreds of true-born East Anglians.

People who could trace their forebears back to the time of the earliest Saxon, Jute and Angle settlers, and who made this fair land theirs after the Roman legions had departed.

Sir Edward Wykham, he of this parish, and his two sons, another named Edward and the youngest named Edmund, stood against the bishop. Good Saxon names, for good Saxon men.

Their rebellion may have been 300 years after the Conquest, but folk memory lingers in these here parts.

Men, and boys, from many nearby villages and headed up by their liege-lords and noble families, joined the rebels at North Walsham. Neither Sir Edward nor either of his sons survived the battle.

After their defeat, the 'Fighting Bishop' exacted his revenge upon the rebels.

He couldn't kill every survivor, as that would leave no one to gather in the ripening crops, nor to sow the seed and farm the land for the next few years' rotation of crops.

But he had to stamp down on the peasants and decided to make an example of the villages in the land held by Sir Edward Wykham. The choice of whose lands to rent asunder was seemingly made by simply sticking a pin in a list.

Retribution was swift.

The menfolk from the major settlement on the south side of the river in the vicinity of the church were spared for labour in the fields. Those on the north side were not so lucky.

And here the record of the Peasants' Revolt in this part of the country, so diligently transcribed from lost sources by the Victorian clerk, ended.

All that remained were some scribbles at the bottom of the page, the sort of thing you would do nowadays on a piece of scrap paper when you're hanging on the telephone waiting to talk to someone from one of the utility companies.

Lines. Dots. Random letters in no particular order.

Just scribbles.

No explanation as to the villagers' actual fate. Nothing about Sir Edward's surviving family. Nothing about the 'Fighting Bishop'.

Interesting story, agreed. It would make a decent documentary, and I'd probably watch it.

But what was so exciting that it got Jacko acting like a kid on Christmas Eve?

"Have you finished yet?" Jacko called over from the porch door.

"I'll be straight there."

One more roll-up before going back in, something told me it might be a while before I got another chance.

I couldn't find him anywhere and didn't want to call out. Not in a church.

Even though churches weren't my thing, this should be a quiet and peaceful place, and although the building appeared empty, I bet someone, somewhere, would hear me and be offended if I started bellowing.

It wasn't completely quiet though. Hearing a scratching, sort of scrabbling, noise in the large alcove area opposite the one in which we had found the record book, I walked over and was confronted by a stack of chairs moving towards me at pace, seemingly under its own steam.

I stepped to one side, half out of shock and half out of a sense of self-preservation.

I could see the headline now in the parish council newsletter: *'Non-believer struck down in church by holy stack of chairs.'*

The haunted chairs stopped, and Jacko stepped out from behind them, a questioning look in his eyes.

He shrugged and then took the book from under my arm, opened it and pointed to the dots and lines at the foot of the page.

Turning on the spot, he walked over to where the stack of chairs had been, and getting to his knees he again pointed, but this time to a stone plinth at floor level.

Then, crawling along the floor, to another stone plinth, then crawling again he pointed to one more.

This was the very same alcove that I had worked in, and I was pleased to note that the repaired stone around the window still looked good.

Then I twigged. That was where I'd seen the pattern before. The pattern of dots and cross-hatched lines.

Not just on the rubbings Jacko had made from the entrance to the pit. And not just in the record book.

The first time I had come across the curious markings was here, on the three sections of stone plinth, in the church.

Obviously I was unaware of what I was looking at back then, and although I don't remember exactly, I probably thought they were just tooling marks left by a careless stonemason. Or maybe an apprentice had been given a small area to work on.

Over the next few hours we pieced together a story, remarkable insofar as it had remained hidden for so long.

There was nothing particularly complex about the cypher. Nowadays our brains are no doubt wired differently than those of our forebears.

We use computers and many of us like crosswords or sudoku puzzles, so working out a cypher made of fairly simple dot and line combinations wouldn't prove too difficult for most people.

But, like all good cyphers, you need the key.

And the key was in the record book.

We soon realised that the scribbles in the book were a copy of the marks incised on the stone plinths. With one huge difference. One that the Victorian clerk who had transcribed them had overlooked.

He had first copied the dots and lines exactly as they appeared on the stone plinths, and then written his decipherment below.

His workings were a jumble of letters, and although they didn't form any immediately recognisable words, there were several places where there was the hint of a word.

The Victorian clerk had done the hard yards, and he had virtually cracked it, but it became much clearer when Jacko realised that the cypher would have been created based on Middle English, the version of our language as it would have been written and spoken seven centuries ago.

We were then well away, as Jacko's studies of the type of medieval writing often found in church records really came to the fore.

Within minutes he had established all the vowels, and before noon we had decoded all three sections of the markings on the stone plinths.

Some words just couldn't be made out, neither in translation nor syntax, but the gist was that immediately after the Peasants' Revolt the men from one of the villages had been taken away and never returned, with no detail given as to their fate.

So that concurred with the record book.

Jacko then checked our codebreaking methodology against the rubbings from the cill of the entrance shaft to the pit.

Bingo.

According to Jacko, Middle English had many spoken dialects and written divergences, so based on the word and sentence structure deciphered from the stone plinths, it became obvious that the same hand had carved the dots and lines on the cill of the entrance shaft to the pit.

Jacko found an unused room at the rear of the adjacent church hall, and we erected a foldaway table to work at.

Each sheet of the rubbings from the stone cill around the pit entrance shaft was numbered, so we laid them out in order and within an hour we had worked out the premise of what the dots and lines were telling us.

Another hour, and after checking some key points on my tablet, we had more detail to work with.

The coded text from the rim of the pit revealed that the pit was reused by the local villagers to store their grain and surplus produce.

This would have been before the builders of the Abbey had diverted the stream to fill their fishponds - thereby silting the riverbed further downstream - and before the pit started to fill with flood water.

Recently completed research, which Jacko had taken part in, had shown that the Abbey was built by the same group of masons as the church, which was another pointer to the same hand having carved the dots and lines in the church, and around the entrance to the pit.

The message on the cill around the pit entrance was strange in that it most definitely had pagan undertones, and the parallels of a medieval builder being associated with carved stone in both a Christian place of worship and a pagan storage pit were not lost on us.

A lot of this was old hat to Jacko as he had covered Medieval History in his studies, but I found it fascinating.

A further hour of research on the internet and we were reading about how not all those living outside the larger urban centres during the early medieval period embraced Christianity, and many still turned to the old ways and traditions of the countryside.

Witch burning happened for a reason - not necessarily because there really were witches, but because people believed there were.

Jacko went to collect a couple of burgers from the pub, and as the search pages were still open on my tablet, I took the opportunity to read up about pagan traditions, especially those that have survived, albeit with different anniversary dates and names.

Mumming, Yule Log burning, Midsummer's Eve, the Green Man, May Pole dancing. And a few more to boot.

There was one tradition, however, which stood out from the surprisingly long list.

Whilst I knew that the harvest festival tended to happen at the end of September, I had never quite worked out why some of the local farmers started to prepare for it so early.

Over the last few days, as in previous years, I had noticed sheaves of barley outside their farm entrance gates and corn dolls tied to fences and lamp posts.

There's nothing quite like preparing in advance, but this was a bit early.

One word which kept popping up was *Lughnasadh*, which was the harvest festival in honour of Lugh, one of the most prominent Celtic pagan gods.

Interestingly, among other associations, Lugh was often given the attributes of a master craftsman and builder.

Early Christianity also developed a tradition of celebrating the cereal harvest, known as 'Loaf Mass', derived from the story of Beowa, a figure in Anglo-Saxon paganism associated with farming and agriculture.

I'd never come across the character called Beowa, but had heard of the next name in the article.

John Barleycorn.

Apparently, many medieval historians view the story of Beowa as the origin of the John Barleycorn tradition from Old English folklore, and they are often considered to be one and the same.

As I turned to the section on John Barleycorn, Jacko returned with our food - two burgers each – and, I noted, a few cans of beer. Good bloke.

He played mother and set out the table, whilst I continued reading.

I read the John Barleycorn folk poem, twice, and agreed with the assessment made by the writer of the article that the story surrounding the suffering, death, and resurrection of John Barleycorn - and the reviving effects of drinking his blood - have obvious Christian parallels.

So here we have several ancient traditions merging until the boundaries are foggy and indistinct, yet sharply focused on the recurring life cycle of all things.

The Celtic Lugh and his association with the craft of building, the Anglo-Saxon Beowa central to the celebration of farming and agriculture, and the medieval John Barleycorn rooted in connotations of the Christian liturgy.

I went through my findings with Jacko as we ate our late lunch. I couldn't eat a second burger and didn't want a beer yet.

The parallels between the various traditions were what stood out most.

Those, and the date.

The Celtic festival of Lughnasadh was held on August 1st.

The early Christian celebration known as 'Loaf Mass', also held on August 1st.

The Anglo-Saxons had a similar festival based on the story of Beowa. On August 1st.

So, three distinct traditions celebrating the first cereal harvests of the year.

Halfway between the summer solstice and the autumn equinox. On August 1st.

During the early medieval period many people still followed the old ways, still honoured the countryside, and still looked to the pagan story of Beowa.

They renamed the already ancient tradition of giving thanks for past harvests and seeking blessings for the next crop.

They called it Lammas Sabbat.

And today was August 1st.

"So, all that stuff on the internet, do you know what it reminds me of?"

Jacko shook his head. "No, what?"

"That cult movie from the 1970's."

"What movie?" He looked at me, confused.

"*The Wicker Man*."

"Nah. I don't know that one."

"Sure you do! The one about the pagan ceremonies on a remote Scottish island."

He still looked confused.

"The one with that bloke out of *Callan*, you know, the movie about spies," I tried to explain.

"What, pagan spies on a Scottish island?" He was really confused now.

"No. The actor out of *Callan* was in *The Wicker Man*. He gets burnt at the end."

"Ah!" the penny had dropped, "the film where that blonde actress gets her kit off."

Some things are lost on some people. A classic movie and he only remembers it because a bit of flesh was on display. Fair game though.

We were sitting in my truck, having only just arrived at Lammas Land.

I know we were both feeling a bit daft, and I guess by trying to act normal in talking typical bloke stuff, we were trying to compensate for our feelings about the decision we had made earlier.

After all, we were supposed to be two grown men.

Back at the church hall, after we had read up on the pagan traditions and were about to turn the tablet off, I found a site which claimed that even now many rural communities still believed in making offerings.

Normally an offering of bread baked from the first harvest of barley, and a young - or green - beer brewed from the same crop, which it was believed would bring good fortune with the next year's harvest.

I suppose there can't be any harm in hedging your bets.

If the rain doesn't come, the sun is clouded over, and the fertilisers don't work, then an offering, or two, should do the trick.

I didn't mean to take the piss, but this was the 21st century after all.

Jacko seemed to be more in tune with this sort of thing than I was, which was surprising really, as he was a churchgoer.

I could understand how the old people who farmed these lands in the past would believe that making offerings could help with a good crop, as that's how their society had evolved, and their individual and collective livelihood was so dependent on a good harvest.

I realised that, by default, the implication was that they believed not making offerings would have led to the opposite outcome.

It was at that point in our journey back in time that Jacko got a bit weird.

"Perhaps we ought to do that."

"What?" I didn't follow.

"You know," he seemed a bit embarrassed, "make an offering."

"Make an offering? Who to? Of what? And why?"

I think I'd blown his little brain with so many questions at once.

"You don't really believe all that, do you?"

"Well, in a way. Yes," he blustered, "sort of."

"In a way?" Me, being all incredulous. "And sort of?"

"Okay, so what about all the weird stuff that's been happening?" He'd turned to face me at that point, all serious. And Jacko very rarely does serious.

"The lights and the noises that woman in the pub told us about. The stuff happening at people's houses. The road accident and the disappearing casualty." He was starting to sound a little edgy.

"And what about you?"

"What about me?" I defended myself. Although I wasn't sure against what.

"Oh, come on!" he virtually snorted. "Your sightings. Visions. Whatever you call them."

I was confused now. Was he on the attack?

"You know it wasn't me yesterday - in the field. You saw something, and probably more than once. And I bet you've had strange feelings as well."

Too bloody true, and I was having one right now.

"What do you mean - 'as well'?" I looked him in the eye. "Have you?"

"Nah!" He was more composed now. "Just a bit of the heebie-jeebies, that's all."

I then had one of my not-so-great ideas. I didn't like to see my mate all stressed out.

"Look, why don't we head over there and leave something?" I couldn't believe what I was saying.

"We have a spare burger bun - that's bread. Well sort of. And I haven't had my beer, so we can leave that as well."

As he turned his head to look away, I'm sure I detected a slight rise and fall of his shoulders.

Then, turning his head back towards me, his head cowed, all he said was, "Thanks, mate."

And that's how we came to be here. Again.

Two grown men, and however ridiculous this made us feel, we were going to leave an offering of a bread roll and a can of beer.

Jacko placed the roll on the area of filled-in earth above the pit. I don't know why, but it didn't seem right to leave a can of beer, so I poured the contents over the earth around the bread roll.

We both shuffled a bit, not quite sure if either of us should say anything.

Job done.

Then I noticed the patch of mist on the other side of the field. Not a large patch, but in the middle I could make out a figure.

I hadn't noticed anyone earlier.

They were doing nothing. Just standing there. In the mist.

Jacko sidled up to me.

"What's up?"

"Look, over there." I nodded in the direction of the mist.

"Who's that then?"

"You can see the figure then?" I had to refer to them as a figure, as I couldn't make out whether it was a man or woman.

Either way, even through the mist I could see they were wearing what looked like a heavy coat, or cloak, with a hood. Not really the type of thing for a hot summer's day.

"Yeah!" He looked at me as if I was daft. "Not clearly though. I didn't know the forecast was for mist today."

We both stood there, just staring.

Then the figure raised an arm and pointed a finger at the chest area on their coat.

Then pointed at us.

Bugger. I knew it was the authorities when I saw them yesterday. They were onto me.

I was sweating and had to calm myself down.

"What do you reckon?" I half-whispered to Jacko. "The VAT man ?"

He knows that I sail close to the wind in my relationship with all things Government.

"Doubt it. Not on a Sunday."

Well, it could be. The country doesn't stop running at the weekend. Unless of course you want something from them.

"It could be the council. Checking up on your land drain stuff."

He made a good point.

Yep. I bet it's the council.

I ought to be on my best behaviour then. Nothing to hide. Except for the sodding great pit under our feet.

"Do you reckon they know about the pit?" Jacko had read my mind.

"Dunno," I shrugged, "they might do."

Now I was feeling worried.

Especially if it was them I'd seen yesterday, and particularly if they had just witnessed our daft little ritual with the burger bun and the tinnie.

They might be testing me. To see if I could be trusted.

"Oh, bollocks!" Jacko, sounding defeated.

"What?"

"I was going to tell you. Honest!"

"Tell me what?" As if I hadn't got enough to think about at the moment.

I looked over towards the figure, still indistinct within the mist.

Unmoving, like a statue.

Where were the pigeons when you needed them?

Well, there's revelations . . . and then, there's revelations.

And Jacko certainly knew how to make a revelation.

I knew he'd been acting a bit cagey ever since yesterday afternoon - after we had pumped out the pit.

And he was particularly nervy yesterday evening, at the pub.

He admitted that he had come back here - to Lammas Land - earlier this morning.

So that accounted for the bad telephone reception when we spoke.

Apparently, whilst looking for the bone fragments yesterday afternoon, he'd discovered something else.

Was that in the same area where he'd had a pee? Urgh!

Anyway, he'd rummaged away and found a piece of metalwork, which he had hidden behind the cricket scoreboard.

A piece of metalwork!

What sort of metalwork? Were we talking silver, or even gold?

He had returned earlier this morning to retrieve it from its hiding place and had it in his pocket. Of course he did!

About four inches long and well preserved, it was heavy for its size, and looked like iron to me.

It was quite plain and didn't strike me as being worth much.

Jacko confirmed my initial thoughts - it was a pin used for securing two pieces of fabric, maybe for securing the flap on a skirt or a cloak.

He reckoned it was probably cast into the pit back in medieval times as part of a pagan ceremony dedicated to the water spirits to ensure a good harvest, or perhaps to stop the floodwater from rising in the pit.

A type of votive offering.

I couldn't argue with his logic. It sounded plausible to me.

All I could think was that it was no wonder the council had set loose their snoopers - they thought I was some sort of treasure hunter. Or a desecrator of ancient monuments.

Or a bastard 'night hawk' grave robber!

Same thing all round.

Well, it had to be reported. We had to 'fess up.

But hang on. That would mean a paper trail.

What if we just put it back? That was Jacko's brilliant idea.

Surprising really, that he would give it up, just like that. I needed to think.

I slipped the pin into my pocket, rolled a cigarette, lit up, inhaled heavily, and looked over towards the figure.

He, for I was now sure in my mind that it was a bloke, was looking straight at me.

I don't know how I knew that, as his image was still blurred by the mist, and under the rim of the hood all I could see was deep shadow, with no facial features visible.

He raised his arm, just as before, and again pointed a finger at his chest - exactly where a pin would be used to secure the flap of a cloak.

He then pointed towards the setting sun.

So, he must know we had the pin, why else indicate where it would be used?

And the sun, what was that all about?

Was he telling us to put it back before the end of the day? That must be it.

Feeling the weight of the pin in my pocket, it occurred to me that if it really was a votive offering from the past - then it could equally become a votive offering today.

I glanced up towards the figure.

Gone.

He knew that we'd got the message. There was no need for him to hang around, as he'd probably got some other poor sap to go and put the frighteners on before the day was over.

The shadows were lengthening, and the sun would be below the horizon soon.

I reckoned we only had a couple of hours at most.

Jacko had finished hooking the rope to the winch on the truck bumper.

"Same process as before then?" he asked.

"Yep. It worked yesterday, so no reason to suppose it won't work now." I pushed my shovel into the mound of earth.

Jacko walked over, pulled it out and took over where I had left off.

I slumped down on the mound and wriggled to make a more comfortable seat.

Popping the lid of my tobacco tin, I removed a cigarette I had rolled earlier.

I lit up, and watched Jacko finish off the last section of the shallow trench.

I was glad he had taken over as, quite honestly, I felt knackered. Both in body and in mind.

I guessed it must be the exertion of yesterday, and the late night and early morning. It catches up with you in the end.

Hopefully, we could get this done quickly and maybe a pint to finish the day off with.

Twenty minutes later and the winch was pulling the slab back.

We left the rope tied around the slab, ready to pull it back later.

"So, do you want to throw it in - or do you want me to?" I asked him.

"You've still got it in your pocket, so you might as well." He didn't seem too pleased, as he kicked the rope into a loose coil on the ground.

"Are you still okay with this?" I took a swig from my bottle of water, then tossed it down on the coiled rope.

"What?" He stood there with his arms crossed. "Am I still okay with me having to give up something I've found so that you can stay in the council's good books ?" He most definitely wasn't still okay with this.

"Yeah, but we agreed. Anyway, it was your idea to put it back!"

"Okay! Don't go on about it. Just do it. I'll move the truck to the other side ready to pull the slab back in place."

And with that he stomped off, with a face like a dog licking pee off stinging nettles.

Let him go, I thought. He'll be fine later. Nothing that a couple of pints wouldn't put right.

That image in my mind made me feel thirsty again, and I reached down for my bottle of water.

I really don't know how it happened - I guess that my feet must have got tangled in the rope.

There I was, swigging back water and watching the sun getting lower in the sky, and now here I was, sitting in a puddle of muddy water looking up at the same sky through the pit's narrow entrance shaft.

I checked myself over, nothing seemed broken, although I had cracked my elbow on the way down, and that was smarting now.

Amazing really that I hadn't done anything more serious, considering the drop.

The rain from last night's storm had found a way in and turned the floor into a muddy sludge.

It was less than a foot deep but had softened the mud sufficiently to break my fall.

However, my glasses had fallen off and I was struggling to focus with any degree of clarity.

Thankfully I saw a glint from the metal frames - within arm's reach.

They were lying in the surface film of liquid mud. Filthy.

I tried to clean the lenses on my shirt, but that didn't help much.

I needed to get Jacko's attention, and the last I saw of him he was heading towards the truck. I cupped my hands around my mouth and directed my call towards the circle of visible sky. No reply.

Then again. Still nothing.

He must have gone for a pee, like he did yesterday when I needed pulling up.

That bloke must have a bladder the size of a thimble.

The water was settling after my fall, with the mud particles sinking.

So I swirled the glasses in the top layer of ever so slightly cleaner water, and then shook them.

A bit better, and that would have to do. But they were ruined.

I could now make out the rope dangling about two feet below the point where the curved walls and the entrance shaft met. Still too high for me to reach though.

As I stood, my right ankle gave way beneath me. Obviously, I hadn't landed as well as I thought.

I winced with the stab of pain.

Odd. No echo from my whimper.

I made a clucking noise. Still no sound bouncing back at me.

The interior was curved. Did that have a cancelling effect on noises? I wished I'd paid more attention in school physics lessons.

The air inside the pit was very still - as I would have expected in an underground chamber.

Not just still, but heavy. Oppressive.

And even though the water ingress was less than 24 hours ago, it felt dank, mouldy . . . and dead.

I didn't like it in here.

There were several niches cut into the wall, presumably for storage of perishable crops, or maybe for candles.

I decided that I would place the pin in one. Which I did.

And, as with the bread and beer earlier, I didn't know if I should say a few words.

I didn't bother, as I just wanted to get out.

I noticed that the other niches were roughly 18 inches apart and staggered vertically.

A medieval climbing wall. I smiled to myself.

Even now, I still had a sense of humour. A lot of good it was doing me though.

Of course, people must have come in and out of the pit to store and then later retrieve their crops. But why not use a ladder?

Perhaps they did, but it had rotted away.

Anyway, I could use the niches to reach the rope.

I pulled myself up one niche after another until my right foot was in the third niche from the surface of the mud, my left foot - taking most of my weight - in the second, and both hands were grasping the lip of the sixth.

As I reached for the rope, right in front of me I noticed some etched lines on the chalk wall.

Steadying myself with the rope grasped in my left hand and my right still having a good hold, I could see that the lines were more like shallow incised engravings, albeit quite crude and basic in design.

The sun must be getting quite low now, as the light penetrating the entrance shaft was dimmer than when I had fallen in.

There were three smaller engravings around a larger central one.

The smaller ones were each similar - a triangle with a cross in the centre set over either a pig, a human skull or what I took to be a horned devil.

The largest engraving looked like a representation of a hole in the ground with human stick figures in and around it. The ones on the outside had what looked like shields and swords.

I tried to manoeuvre myself for a closer inspection, and as I did so my weight shifted to my right leg.

The stabbing pain in my ankle was excruciating, and I felt myself toppling.

Grasping for the rope with both hands, I reached it just as my leg gave way beneath me.

I'm sure it was for only a fraction of a second, but I seemed to hang there for an age - both arms wrapped around the rope and legs flailing.

Next thing, splosh. On my arse in the mud again.

For a few horrible seconds I thought the whole length of rope would end up in my lap. But thankfully it jerked to a stop. I remembered it was still tied around the slab.

As I stood to check again for injuries, I trod on something solid in the mud, something that hadn't been there before my climb.

I reached into the mud and felt a smooth, round object with several holes in it.

I laughed out loud as I tried to imagine what a bowling ball was doing down here.

The mud was sucking at it, and I had to stick a couple of fingers in one of the holes and rock it from side to side so that it came loose.

Well, that really freaked me out, and I could hear myself gibbering like a lunatic.

Standing there, I must have looked like Hamlet chatting away to poor Yorick.

My fingers were in the cavity at the base of the skull where the spine would have joined, leaving those dead, mud-filled sockets staring up at me.

If I'd had the wherewithal, I would have thrown it down, but my attention was now focused intently on an outcrop of mud across the other side of the pit.

I hadn't taken much notice of it before, as even though it was six feet wide and stood at least three feet above the waterline and projected a couple of feet from the wall, it was nowhere near the entrance shaft, so afforded no use at all as a way out.

I must have released the pressure on something when I removed the skull, as the mud pile started burbling.

Then, with no warning at all, it collapsed and slid into the water. It had probably been there for centuries.

Whilst I most definitely didn't want to be here, I was somewhat morbidly fascinated by the skull, and the pile of mud which was now gradually dissolving in the water.

Would it reveal what had been buried? Treasure - maybe.

But no. Sliding out of the remains of the mud pile were bones. Human bones. And lots of them.

I don't know what bones go where in the body, but I do know that when you count eight skulls, nine including the one I had just dropped, then there are the remains of nine people.

I felt sick. I felt alone. I felt scared.

I'd left my watch in the truck, so I had no idea how late it was, but it did seem to be getting ever dimmer in here.

I looked around me and the only light coming in from the shaft was striking the upper part of the wall on the other side.

There was enough light to make out shapes, but not details. No problem though, as Jacko would be here soon.

Surely.

I caught hold of the rope and tied a bowline around my chest and under my arms in readiness.

Movement. Over the other side.

From memory that's only about 25 feet away.

Something moved again - in the shadows.

Probably my shadow - but then I reminded myself that there was no light source behind me.

It moved again. I tried to focus and once again wiped my shirt sleeve over the mud smeared lenses.

The shadow, for that's what it looked like, was definitely moving.

Within the shadow, the darkness was swirling like a black fog.

Rooted to the spot with mouth agape, I stared as, before me, the whole mass seemed to coalesce from a nebulous collection of individual areas of darkness into a more defined shape.

Emerging from the gloom, seemingly from the very surface of the mud-covered walls, the shape slowly took on a gentle swaying and rhythmic motion.

I could feel dribble trickling from the corner of my mouth, yet I hadn't the courage to wipe it away.

I didn't even dare to blink.

Part of me was trying to apply a rational explanation to what I was seeing.

Was I really seeing anything at all?

Was it just shadows?

Had I cracked my head when I fell?

Was I concussed?

All I knew was that the shape before me was now billowing at the centre, like a blanket pegged to a washing line on a good drying day. Nothing gentle or rhythmic about it any more.

The darker than dark shape at the centre now seemed to have taken on another form.

A cloak, with a hood.

A cloak, covering the shape of a person.

A cloak without a fastening, threatening to flap open to reveal whatever was beneath.

Without a fastening - without a pin?

My throat was so dry as I tried to call out that all I could emit was a harsh, rasping gurgle.

My breathing was becoming laboured, with probably centuries of mould spores now lodged in my lungs, and the dizziness and nausea were getting worse.

This must all be in my mind, I thought. I was sure it could be explained away by ordinary, level-headed, and rational thoughts.

But my eyes just couldn't look away from the thing in front of me, now within touching distance, as the hood of the cloak started to gently fall away.

It started to raise its head, and in the swirling darkness I made out the chalky white of the lower jaw of a skull.

All thoughts of a rational explanation left me, as I slammed my eyes shut, unwilling to look any more at what was slowly being revealed.

Then the most beautiful sound I could imagine.

The cough of a motor.

I felt the rope tighten under my armpits and around my upper chest, and then I was rising - not fast, but fast enough.

As I ascended, the warm evening air was gently wafting around the entrance shaft, and opening my eyes I dared to look down, into the pit.

Which was empty.

The motor on the winch continued to reel me in. It didn't stop.

Why didn't Jacko stop it?

I was being dragged along the ground, like a lassoed cowboy in one of those old Westerns.

Managing to slip one arm out of the bowline around my chest, I rolled the other way and then was free.

I lay there for a few seconds before remembering what I had witnessed - or thought I had witnessed.

The thought of it, though, was enough to get me up and stagger towards the truck.

My ankle hurt like hell. Can a person still run with a broken ankle?

My hands were shaking so much that I scratched the paintwork around the driver's door lock, more in five seconds than I had in the three years that I'd owned the truck.

I tumbled into the driver's seat, slammed the door, and punched down on the auto-lock.

No one was getting in here.

I sat there, leaning on the steering wheel, just for a minute.

Thankfully, my dizziness was clearing, and I was breathing a lot better.

Irrespective of the state of my lungs, I had to have a cigarette.

One day I'll give up. But that day was not today.

The cigarette helped calm me down, as I tried to process the events of the last couple of days.

Most of it was jumbled in my mind, but I did recall the images carved into the chalk high up in the pit.

I'd only seen them for half a minute or so, but my recollection was quite clear.

Opening the glove compartment, I took out my spare pair of glasses. I always keep them in there as today wasn't the first time I had ruined a pair on a job.

I noticed Jacko's bag in the footwell and reached in for his spiral-bound notepad. I had a pencil tucked under the driver's sun-visor and, turning to a new page, I started to sketch the images of the engravings.

An old girlfriend once taught me how to use word association to remember lists and such things.

I could still recite every King and Queen of England, every Prime Minister, and every winner of the English Premier League and the old First Division.

If nothing else, it's a good party trick.

In my mind, I saw a sausage being eaten by a pirate wearing a Manchester United football strip.

Simple to reconstruct.

A pig. A human skull. A horned devil.

The triangle with the cross at its centre was easy enough to recall.

Equally, the largest engraving I remembered just as it was - a hole in the ground with human stick figures in and around it, with the ones on the outside looking like soldiers.

It was quite clear to me what all of this meant, and it made me sad and angry at the same time.

The ever so brave 'Fighting Bishop' had the men from Wickham Magna, north of the river, thrown into the pit as a reprisal for their part in the Peasants' Revolt.

They couldn't write so they scratched pictorial representations of what had happened. And of who was guilty.

The triangle with a cross at the centre - a bishop's mitre.

And they were calling him a pig, the bringer of death, in league with the Devil.

Did they drown, suffocate, or starve?

Probably a combination of all three. It was horrible.

With no independent witnesses, the story of the plague killing off the villagers would have been easy to concoct and perpetuate.

I closed my eyes and couldn't help but see them trying to escape by digging out the niches - probably with their bare hands - and use them as I had tried to.

But the stone slab above them did its macabre job.

I wiped my eyes, and as I replaced my glasses, I noticed a can of beer in Jacko's bag.

Thinking that I'd have a quick one - especially after the crap I'd just been through - I reached in for the can.

A small clear plastic bag had got entangled in the ring pull.

It was one of those coin bags used in banks, and inside I could see a dull metal object.

I opened the bag and tipped the contents into my palm.

It was a lightly engraved and clearly very old ring - possibly silver.

Straight away I knew what I was looking at - and what it meant.

I think I knew what I had seen, earlier, in the pit - but the problem was that I didn't know if I wanted to believe what I'd seen.

If there really was a figure, and not just a shadow within my imagination, then I bet it wasn't happy about Jacko keeping the ring.

All they wanted was the return of the pin and the ring - that's why they couldn't settle.

No wonder Jacko was, sort of, okay with the return of the pin - he still had the ring.

The prat.

Was that why the figure kept extending its finger - kept pointing? To replace the ring which should have been on its finger.

It would have to go back.

The sun was close to disappearing, so I turned the key, started the engine and flicked on the headlights.

A quick three-point turn and the area around the pit entrance was illuminated.

No ceremony this time. No big gestures.

I limped as close to the entrance as I felt comfortable with and threw the ring in - from ten feet away, and even though I could hear nothing above the engine noise, I imagined it rattling against the inside of the shaft.

I contemplated leaving the pit uncovered until the morning, but the Gods help anyone who fell in there now.

I didn't want to get any closer to that hole in the ground than I had to, and I was glad that we had left the rope tied around the slab earlier.

Pulling the rope up, I hooked the other end to the winch; I then heard what sounded like someone calling my name - but so far off. The engine noise didn't help.

He'd heard the truck, or he'd seen the headlights, and now wanted a lift back to the village.

I got in the truck, switched on the winch motor, and watched the rope tighten as the slab was slowly pulled over the entrance shaft.

Hang on!

How did the motor start up when I was pulled out - if the truck was locked?

And why hadn't Jacko turned the truck around?

Mate of mine or not - he had a lot of questions to answer.

It took me about ten minutes to shovel the earth over the slab and replace the turf.

There it was again. It sounded like my name being called - this time closer but muted, sort of deadened.

I decided to give Jacko a bit more time - but, if he wasn't here within the next five minutes then he could bloody well walk back.

Back in the truck I rolled another cigarette and was pleased that at least the pit was sealed again, and this time hopefully forever.

Slowly drawing in the smoke, I thought about part of the old folk poem I had read earlier in the day on one of the websites.

Was that really this morning? It seemed so long ago now.

'They filled up a darksome pit

with water to the brim,

they heav'd in John Barleycorn.

There, let him sink or swim!'

I reached over for my watch on the dashboard. Five minutes up - time to go.

I must have been hearing things, but I wondered where Jacko had got to?

He must have got really moody about that pin, and I couldn't wait to see his face when I told him about the ring.

Ah, well!

The little git couldn't hide forever.

Thank you for reading my book, I hope you enjoyed it.
If you have time, could you please leave a review on the Amazon site.

You can find out more about my series of books at :

Andrew Fordham : Amazon Author Page

I really enjoy engaging with readers of my books, and have set up a blog page on my website which I invite you to join.

Over time, I will give insights into my writing process - such as characterisation, settings, and plot research, and will also use the Blog page to keep readers informed of my upcoming new books and series.

You can sign up at :

Andrew Fordham : Blog

I hope to see you there !

Printed in Great Britain
by Amazon